DONATED BY THE:

Hillsboro

Education

Association's

"BOOK SWAP AND ADOPT"

Tales

Selected By Eva Moore
Illustrated by Thea Kliros
Cover by Tom Newsom

SCHOLASTIC INC.

New York   Toronto   London   Auckland   Sydney

If you purchased this book without a cover, you should be aware that this book is stolen property. It was reported as "unsold and destroyed" to the publisher, and neither the author nor the publisher has received any payment for this "stripped book."

No part of this publication may be reproduced in whole or in part, or stored in a retrieval system, or transmitted in any form or by any means, electronic, mechanical, photocopying, recording, or otherwise, without written permission of the publisher. For information regarding permission, write to Scholastic Inc., Attention: Permissions Department, 555 Broadway, New York, NY 10012.

ISBN 0-590-21692-9

Compilation copyright © 1997 by Scholastic Inc.
Illustrations © 1997 Scholastic Inc.
All rights reserved. Published by Scholastic Inc.
SCHOLASTIC and associated logos are trademarks and/or registered trademarks of Scholastic Inc.

12 11 10 9 8 7 6 5 4 3 2   7 8 9/9 0 1 2/0

Printed in the U.S.A.   40

First Scholastic printing, November 1997

Contents

Counting the Days

How many days to Christmas?
Forty, thirty, and then —
Twenty-five, twenty, seventeen,
Fourteen, eleven, ten.

Nine eight seven — six five four —
Three days, two days slowly go.
But the last day before Christmas
Is — slow — slow — slow.

James S. Tippett

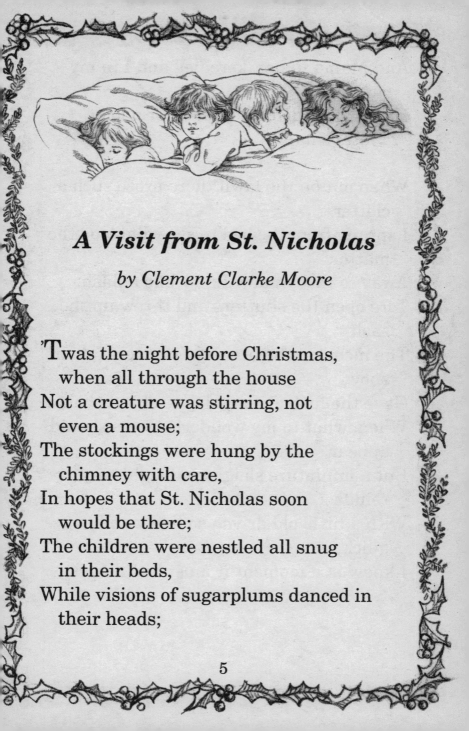

A Visit from St. Nicholas

by Clement Clarke Moore

'Twas the night before Christmas,
    when all through the house
Not a creature was stirring, not
    even a mouse;
The stockings were hung by the
    chimney with care,
In hopes that St. Nicholas soon
    would be there;
The children were nestled all snug
    in their beds,
While visions of sugarplums danced in
    their heads;

And Mama in her 'kerchief, and I in my
    cap,
Had just settled our brains for a long
    winter's nap;

When out on the lawn there arose such a
    clatter,
I sprang from the bed to see what was the
    matter.
Away to the window I flew like a flash,
Tore open the shutters and threw up the
    sash.
The moon on the breast of the new-fallen
    snow,
Gave the lustre of midday to objects below,
When, what to my wondering eyes should
    appear,
But a miniature sleigh, and eight tiny
    reindeer,
With a little old driver, so lively and
    quick,
I knew in a moment it must be St. Nick.

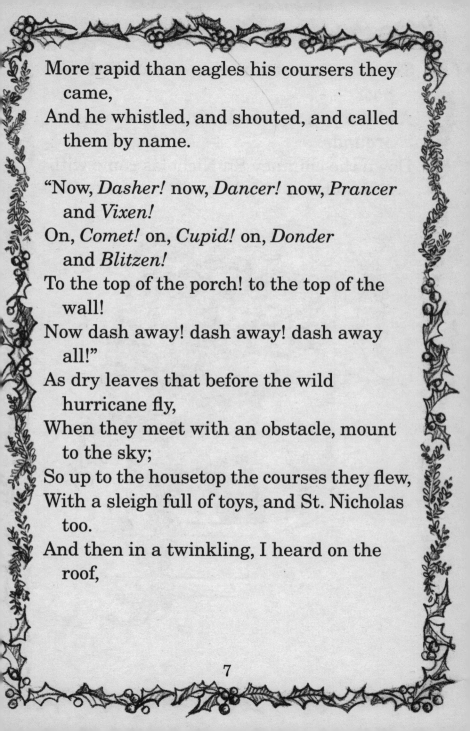

More rapid than eagles his coursers they
    came,
And he whistled, and shouted, and called
    them by name.

"Now, *Dasher!* now, *Dancer!* now, *Prancer*
    and *Vixen!*
On, *Comet!* on, *Cupid!* on, *Donder*
    and *Blitzen!*
To the top of the porch! to the top of the
    wall!
Now dash away! dash away! dash away
    all!"
As dry leaves that before the wild
    hurricane fly,
When they meet with an obstacle, mount
    to the sky;
So up to the housetop the courses they flew,
With a sleigh full of toys, and St. Nicholas
    too.
And then in a twinkling, I heard on the
    roof,

The prancing and pawing of each little
   hoof —
As I drew in my head, and was turning
   around,
Down the chimney St. Nicholas came with
   a bound.

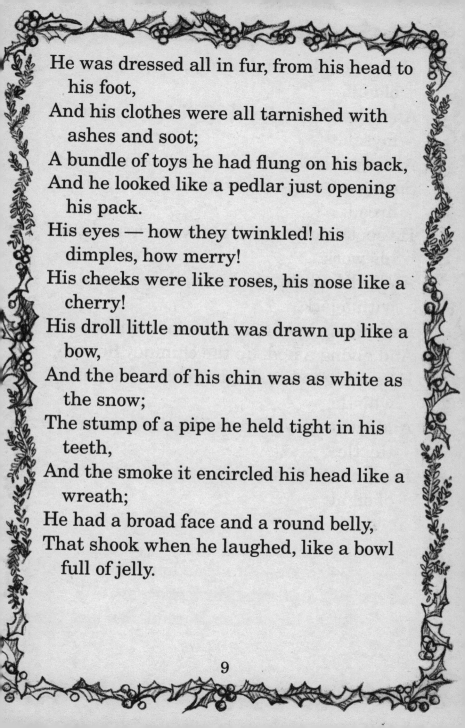

He was dressed all in fur, from his head to
his foot,
And his clothes were all tarnished with
ashes and soot;
A bundle of toys he had flung on his back,
And he looked like a pedlar just opening
his pack.
His eyes — how they twinkled! his
dimples, how merry!
His cheeks were like roses, his nose like a
cherry!
His droll little mouth was drawn up like a
bow,
And the beard of his chin was as white as
the snow;
The stump of a pipe he held tight in his
teeth,
And the smoke it encircled his head like a
wreath;
He had a broad face and a round belly,
That shook when he laughed, like a bowl
full of jelly.

He was chubby and plump, a right jolly
  old elf,
And I laughed when I saw him, in spite of
  myself.
A wink of his eye and a twist of his head,
Soon gave me to know I had nothing to
  dread;
He spoke not a word, but went straight to
  his work;
And fill'd all the stockings; then turned
  with a jerk,
And laying his finger aside of his nose,
And giving a nod, up the chimney he rose;
He sprang to his sleigh, to his team gave a
  whistle,
And away they all flew like the down of a
  thistle.
But I heard him exclaim, ere he drove out
  of sight,

"HAPPY CHRISTMAS TO ALL AND TO ALL A GOOD NIGHT."

The Lost Christmas

Story and pictures by Howard Knotts

It was Christmas afternoon.

The train had slowed down, coasted into the tunnel, and stopped. The last two cars, a hopper with coal and a red caboose, stayed outside the tunnel.

Luke loved the red caboose, but he couldn't watch his train run anymore. He felt hot and dizzy in his head. He put his cheek against the cool wood floor.

Then his mother came and found him there, and his father carried him to bed. As his mother tucked him in, Luke thought, *I don't want to lose Christmas. The day is only half over. If I go to bed, it will just slip away.*

But he had to close his eyes at last because he felt so very tired. *I'll only rest a minute*, he thought. He could hear his mother and father talking, but their voices seemed far away. From somewhere came the sound of rising wind.

Luke opened his eyes and sat up. His bed was moving through a forest! The wind was cool against his face. Leaves were blowing past.

Deer ran along beside him. Luke wanted to touch them, but when he reached out, they ran faster. "I'll run, too," said Luke to himself. He leaped from his bed, and the wind held him high as he began to run on the air!

Above him the stars went rushing past. The wind felt wonderfully cool. Now the deer were far below. Still Luke kept

running, running. *I've never gone so fast,* he thought, *and I'm not even out of breath.*

Past a waterfall he ran, and over a stream. Down he swooped under a bridge and felt spray from the stream on his face. Luke was very happy, and he didn't feel dizzy at all anymore.

On and on he went. He ran past castles and mountains. He ran through clouds and snow.

Finally he stopped and let himself down in a clearing in some woods. The wind was quiet. The night was still. *I must be a long way from home*, Luke thought, and he shivered. Then he saw a railroad track in the grass. It disappeared into a tunnel. Luke wondered where it went.

The tunnel was dark, and Luke was afraid. He thought about turning back, but he did not remember the way he had come.

Then Luke made himself be brave and step into the tunnel's blackness. *Tunnels don't last forever*, he thought, *and I might find a friendly house when I come out on the other side.*

Luke walked and walked for a very long time. He wanted to sit down and rest. At last he saw a light ahead. He strained his eyes to see it. There was a train in the tunnel. And the light came from a red caboose. A bell rang! A whistle blew! Luke ran and pulled himself aboard just as the train started moving.

The train left the tunnel and began to pick up speed. Fields and farms went rushing past. "I'm riding a real caboose!"

shouted Luke. He wished the train would take him on forever. But as it sped onward, Luke began to feel tired and wished for someplace soft to lie down.

Suddenly the train stopped again. There in the grass beside the tracks was his bed! "Just in time," said Luke, who could hardly keep his eyelids open. He climbed into bed and pulled up the covers. Soft white snow-flakes began to fall.

His bed felt cozy and warm. *It's so good to lie down*, Luke thought. Just before he fell asleep, he thought, *If I'm back in my bed, I can't be too far from home.*

The next time Luke opened his eyes he was looking into his mother's face. Sun-shine filled the room. His mother smiled and helped him to sit up. "Taste this," she said. And she fed him delicious soup from a spoon. "You've been very, very ill," she said. "Your father and I were sick with worry. The doctor came. You were burning with fever. We sponged your face with water. At last the fever broke, and now we have you back again."

"The caboose," whispered Luke, between spoonfuls of soup, "the red caboose brought me back. Is it still Christmas?"

"Christmas was three days ago," his mother said. "Now lie back and rest."

"Christmas was three days ago," said Luke to himself. "I lost Christmas!" But before he could feel sad, he began to remember his dream. He remembered the deer and running on the wind; the waterfall and the stars rushing past. He remembered riding the red caboose. Then he smiled, for he remembered his own red caboose was waiting for him still under the Christmas tree.

Words from
an Old Spanish Carol

Shall I tell you who will come
   To Bethlehem on Christmas morn?
Who will kneel them gently down
   Before the Lord new-born?

One small fish from the river,
   With scales of red, red gold,
One wild bee from the heather,
   One gray lamb from the fold,
One ox from the high pasture,
   One black bull from the herd,
One goatling from the far hills,
   One white, white bird.

And many children — God give them
   grace,
Bringing tall candles to light Mary's
   face.

Shall I tell you who will come
   To Bethlehem on Christmas morn?
Who will kneel them gently down
   Before the Lord new-born?

Ruth Sawyer, translator

The Cat in the Manger

by Wendie Old

The cat who lived in the stable behind the inn didn't think it was strange that the woman had chosen to have her baby there. After all, what better place could there be in Bethlehem? The cow and the donkey had their young in the stable. And the dog liked to nurse her litter over in that corner. The cat herself, of course, preferred to have her tiny striped kittens under the manger.

But now . . . she perked up her ears. Where was all that singing coming from — the sky?

When first the shepherds and then three kings came to see the newborn babe, she quickly hid.

Such a fuss over a baby, she thought, blinking her green eyes. She noticed that the mother looked worried.

"Go to sleep, my little one," she sang, patting the baby gently.

But the baby wouldn't go to sleep.

He watched the cows *munch munch*, chewing their cuds.

He watched the dog follow her tail around three times, then flop down for a nap.

He watched the birds fluttering in the rafters.

"Go to sleep, Jesus. Go to sleep, my son," crooned the mother softly.

But the baby wouldn't go to sleep.

He watched the cat wash herself from the tip of her nose to the tip of her tail.

After three last satisfying licks, the cat looked up. The baby was still watching.

I'll just have to show this new mother how to sing a baby to sleep, the cat thought.

She leaped onto the manger and nestled in the straw beside the human baby.

Purrrrrr, she sang and butted the baby gently with her head. *Purrrrr. . . .*

Slowly the baby's eyes closed. The tabby cat purred softly until he fell asleep. Then she curled up beside the baby and slept.

She awoke from her catnap to find the mother stroking her. Head to tail. Head to tail. It felt *sooooo* good. She purred again, butting the hand with her head so the mother's fingers could find that oh-so-itchy spot above her eyebrows.

After that, when the mother wanted her baby to sleep, the cat jumped in the manger and purred.

And if she was at all interested in looking at herself, which she wasn't, she might have noticed that the dark stripes on her forehead had rearranged themselves.

And from that time until this, all tabby cats have had on their foreheads the letter M.

M for Madonna.

M for Mother.

M for the stable cat sharing her wisdom of motherhood with Mary, the Mother of Jesus.

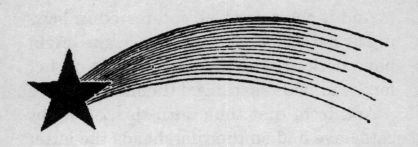

The Story of Old Befana

by Jan Evans-Tiller

Once upon a time, long ago, there lived an old, old woman, older than your father, older than your grandfather. Her name was Befana, and she lived at the end of a road that led nowhere, and everywhere. She lived all alone, though this had not always been so. She once had a husband and a great many children. And she was forever cooking, baking, and cleaning up the house after her large family.

But at the time of this story, her husband was long dead and her children were long gone. But she kept on cooking, baking, and cleaning the house. She even cleaned it when it didn't seem dirty at all!

Sometimes when the weather was fine and people were outside a lot, they could smell the wonderful aroma of Befana's cooking coming from her open kitchen window. "Mmm," they would say. "We smell cinnamon. Befana must be making cookies!"

One evening, as the old woman was sweeping her floor, she heard a most unusual sound, coming closer and closer. She thought at first it was a bird. Then she thought it might be a flute. All of a sudden, the noise stopped — right outside her door! Carefully, Befana opened the door just a crack and peeked out. There, on her doorstep, were three camels, all wearing harnesses with bells — which is where the sound had come from — and all carrying men dressed richly like kings.

"Greetings, Befana," said the oldest and tallest of the three. "We seek the world's most special child, in order to offer our love and respect. That bright star," he said, pointing to the eastern sky, "will lead us to the place where the child dwells. Will you come with us?"

Befana stood still, with her mouth wide-open in surprise. "I'd like to go," she said, "but I have all this work to do. The cooking and the baking, the sweeping and dusting are never done."

Actually, there was really no need for Befana to clean or bake anymore that night. She just did not want to leave her comfortable house. And, to tell you the truth, she was also afraid of riding one of those camels!

The three men left her, however, and turned their camels toward the road. Waving good-bye, they began once again to follow the star in the eastern sky . . . and Befana went back to her sweeping.

"Imagine that," she grumbled. "Wanting me to leave my work and go trotting off into the night! On a camel, of all things!" She finished sweeping and sat down to rest.

As she sat, she thought about the special child the kings were seeking. *I wonder if the kings will think to take some toys*, she thought. She thought about all the toys in the big trunk in her house — the toys her children had played with when they were little. Befana continued to rest and think. *And when my children were little, I was too*

*tired, sometimes, to do the sweeping. I won-
der if the kings will think to take a broom.*

It was now quite late. The old woman
made herself a cup of tea and drank it, put
on her nightgown, and went to bed. But as
she lay there, she continued to think about
the special child. She thought about the
mother and father. And she thought about
the kings on their camels, following a star.

Befana lay on her back for a while. She
turned on her side. Then she stretched,
wriggled her toes, and turned on her other
side. But nothing helped! She could not
sleep. She kept thinking about the child
and the kings.

Finally she got up. "No sense lying here," she grumbled. "Those kings will never remember to take the right things on their journey. They don't know enough about children! I might as well see if I can catch up to them. Oh, how I'd like to see that child!"

Hastily, Befana dressed. Picking up a large sack, she went to the trunk full of toys. She put a ball, a soft cuddly doll, and a tiny wooden horse in her sack; then she took the sack to the kitchen and put in a whole batch of cinnamon cookies. On top of that she put a warm shawl. (*In case the weather changes*, she thought.) Befana tied the sack shut. She picked up her broom from beside the door, stepped outside, and shut the door firmly behind her.

Befana looked up at the eastern sky and began walking, with the star leading her way. *I'll catch up with those kings soon*, she thought.

But she didn't. She began walking faster, and faster, and then she began to run. She

ran so fast she almost seemed to be flying, her sack on her back, and her broom in both hands. For many miles she traveled. Many the towns she visited in her search. Many the children she saw.

Finally, Befana grew tired. She began to go more slowly. She looked carefully at the children in towns through which she traveled, often peering at them through an open window as they slept. Each one seemed special to her, special enough to be the child the three men had spoken of. *Perhaps*, she thought, *the men have already come, greeted the child, and moved on. I think I'll leave something here, just in case this child is the special one.* So she tucked a toy beneath the child's pillow, put some cookies by the bed, and cleaned the child's room with her old broom.

Over and over Befana did this. She never again saw the three men, and she never stopped leaving toys and cookies for all the children she saw in her wanderings.

Surprisingly, her supplies never dwindled at all! She does it to this day. Mothers, lifting their heads and sniffing the air, still say, "Oh, cinnamon! Befana must have been here!" And Befana, looking carefully at the face of each child, still says, "This one certainly seems special. I think I'll leave something, just in case. . . ."

Apple Tree Christmas

by Trinka Hakes Noble

The Ansterburgs lived in the end of an old barn. Underneath, Mrs. Woolly and her lambs moved about, Old Dan bumped in his stall, and Sweet Clover mooed at milking time. On the first floor, Mama cooked on a big black stove, and Papa worked in his woodshop. And above, Katrina and Josie slept in the hayloft. Someday Papa would build them a real house. But for now, living in the barn with the soft animal sounds and sweet smell of hay was just right.

Near the barn was an old apple tree. It was overgrown with wild grapevines, but Papa never cut away the vines because they made a natural ladder to the highest apples. "Besides," he always joked, "I could never separate such close friends."

"Girls, we'll be picking apples soon," said Mama one day.

"Maybe sooner than you think," said Papa. "I heard they got a foot of snow up north."

"Oh, dear," fretted Mama, "winter so soon."

"We'd better get the apples in tomorrow," said Papa.

"And I'll make a big batch of apple butter," said Mama. "You girls should stay home from school to help sort apples."

"Hurray!" shouted Katrina and Josie.

The next morning the ground was white, but even in the snow sorting apples was fun. Some went into a pile for cider and applesauce, some went into baskets for pies, small ones were for their lunch pails, and the bruised ones were for Old Dan. But finding the apples to decorate their Christmas tree was what Katrina and Josie liked the best. All day long they picked and chose until the most beautiful apples of all stood on the stone wall. Then Mama picked the biggest one.

"This will make a nice clove apple for our Christmas dinner table," she said. They wrapped the rest of the apples in cloth, and Papa put them in the bottom of the barn to keep until Christmas.

Now that all the apples were picked, Katrina and Josie could climb the tree as much as they wanted. Every day after school they would play in its branches.

On one side Papa had pulled a thick vine down low enough to make a swing for Josie.

The other side of the tree belonged to Katrina. One limb made a perfect drawing board. She called it her studio. There she would dream and draw until the cold winter sun glowed low behind the trees.

"Time for chores," called Mama as she lit the lantern.

Katrina and Josie ran inside the barn and climbed down the ladder to the animals' stalls. First they shelled corn for the hens, then they fed and watered Old Dan.

Papa was putting Mrs. Woolly and her family in a stall with Old Dan and Sweet Clover.

"Papa, what are you doing?" asked Katrina.

"We'll put the stock together tonight so they can keep warm. You climb up and stuff straw in those holes. It must have dropped twenty degrees in the last hour," said Papa.

Katrina could feel the north wind blowing through the holes in the barn. Papa spread a thick layer of straw around the animals. Then he watered them again because by morning their trough would be frozen solid.

It was cold upstairs, too, but Mama had moved the table close to the stove, and a hot supper of apple fritters and maple syrup soon warmed them up.

That night the blizzard hit with full force. The old barn shook, and its beams creaked as if they were in pain.

In the loft, Katrina woke with a start. She could hear Papa and Mama talking softly below. "Probably be gone by morning," Papa said. So she snuggled closer to Josie and went back to sleep.

But the blizzard got worse and lasted for three days and nights.

On the third night something strange woke Katrina. The wind was howling and the beams were screaming, but there was also a different, more frightening sound — like a million sharp knives slashing the roof, cutting the barn, trying to get in.

Katrina was so frightened that she started to scream, but Mama and Papa were already there, wrapping her up in quilts.

"Papa, what is it?" asked Katrina, shaking with fright.

"Ice storm. We're moving you girls downstairs in case the roof caves in under the weight."

Mama put Katrina and Josie on a feather bed under the table. "Now try to sleep," she said.

But Katrina couldn't fall asleep. The ice storm tore at the barn, and when Mama opened the stove door to add more wood, the firelight made an eerie orange glow.

The next morning was calm. The storm had passed. Katrina was glad until she saw Papa's long face when he came inside.

"Ice storm took the old apple tree," he said.

"But surely the vines would hold it together," said Mama.

"No, it split right down through the middle. I'll chop it up for firewood," said Papa.

Katrina ran to the window and knelt down. Through her tears she saw nothing but a heap of snow and ice and dead branches.

Every morning Papa brought in another pile of firewood and vines from the apple tree. Mama said they should keep busy knitting Papa's Christmas presents. Josie finished Papa's scarf and made one for Mama, too. Katrina worked on Mama's pincushion, but she just couldn't concentrate on knitting Papa's socks while he sawed and hacked away at the apple tree. She had ripped out the heel and started over so many times that she had all but ruined the yarn from Mrs. Woolly.

"Well, I'll miss the old apple tree," said Mama, "but it will keep us warm this long winter."

"Yes, I'm thankful for the firewood," said Papa.

How could he be thankful, thought Katrina. Didn't he know that he was chopping up her studio? Didn't he know he was ruining her drawing board?

The day before Christmas came, Mama

made her clove apple and began baking pies. Papa brought in a fresh pine tree, and they decorated it with the beautiful apples. But to Katrina it just didn't feel like Christmas.

Even when she went to bed on Christmas Eve, Papa was still sawing away at the apple tree.

On Christmas morning their stockings were filled with oranges, wild hickory nuts, black walnuts, and peppermint sticks. Josie gave Papa and Mama their scarves, and Katrina gave Mama the pincushion. But it still didn't feel like Christmas to Katrina.

Then Papa said, "Now my little ones, turn around and close your eyes. No peeking."

First Katrina heard Papa ask Mama to help him. Then she heard him hammering something to the beam, then he dragged something across the floor.

"All right, you can look now," said Mama.

They whirled around.

There, hanging from the beam, was Josie's swing, the very same vine swing from the apple tree. Sitting on the swing was a little rag doll that Mama had made.

Near the swing was a drawing board made from the very same limb that had been Katrina's studio. On the drawing board were real charcoal paper and three sticks of willow charcoal.

Katrina softly touched the drawing board. She wanted to say, How wise and wonderful you are, Papa. Thank you, Papa.

I'll always love you, Papa. But all she could say was, "Oh, Papa."

Papa didn't say anything either. He just handed her the three sticks of charcoal.

Josie began to swing with her doll, and Katrina started to draw. Now she could see how beautiful Mama's clove apple looked on the white tablecloth and how shiny red the apples were on the Christmas tree. Now she could smell the fresh winter pine tree and the warm apple pies.

Now it felt like Christmas.

Presents

I wanted a rifle for Christmas,
  I wanted a bat and a ball,
I wanted some skates and a bicycle,
  But I didn't want mittens at all.
    I wanted a whistle
      And I wanted a kite,
    I wanted a pocketknife
      That shut up tight.
    I wanted some boots
      And I wanted a kit,
But I didn't want mittens one little bit.

I told them I didn't like mittens,
  I told them as plain and plain.
I told them I didn't WANT mittens,
  And they've given me mittens again!

Marchette Chute

Every year at Christmastime, children write letters to Santa Claus. Wouldn't it be great to receive a letter back? Many years ago, some children in England did get letters from the North Pole, from "Father Christmas," as they call Santa in England. The letters were actually written by their own father, who was a famous author. In the letter on the next page, Father Christmas writes about all the trouble he has, thanks to his chief assistant, the North Polar Bear!

A Letter from Father Christmas

by J.R.R. Tolkien

December 1925

I am dreadfully busy this year and not very rich. In fact, awful things have been happening, and some of the presents have got spoilt, and I haven't got the North Polar Bear to help me, and I have had to move house just before Christmas, so you can imagine what a state everything is in.

It all happened like this: One very windy day last November my hood blew off and went and stuck on the top of the North Pole. I told him not to, but the North Polar Bear climbed up to the thin top to get it down — and he did. The pole broke in the middle and fell on the roof of my house, and the North Polar Bear fell through the hole it made into the dining room with my hood over his nose, and all the snow fell off the roof into the house and melted and put out all the fires and ran down into the cellars where I was collecting this year's presents, and the North Polar Bear's leg got broken. He is well again now, but I was so cross with him that he says he won't try to help me again. I expect his temper is hurt and will be mended by next Christmas. . . .

Love from Father Christmas

In the Great Walled Country

by Raymond Alden
Adapted by Eva Moore

Far away up at the north end of the world is a land called The Great Walled Country. It got its name because all around the country is a wall, hundreds of feet thick and hundreds of feet high. The wall is made of ice and never melts, winter or summer. For this reason not many people have ever seen the place.

The land is filled with children, for nobody who lives there ever grows up. The king and queen, the princes, and members of the court may be as old as you please, but they are children, too. They play a great deal of the time, but they make excellent rulers and everyone is pleased with the government.

There are all sorts of curious things about the way they live in The Great Walled Country, but this story is only about their Christmas.

You can just imagine what fun their Christmas must be, so near to the North Pole, with ice and snow everywhere. But that's not all. Grandfather Christmas lives just on the north side of the country, so close that his house leans against the great wall for support. (Grandfather Christmas is his name in The Great Walled Country. Here we might call him Santa Claus.)

Having Grandfather Christmas for a neighbor has many advantages. For one, he takes care of all the Christmas shopping for the children in the Great Walled Country. On Christmas Eve, just before he sets out to deliver presents in the rest of the world, he goes into a huge forest of Christmas trees that grows behind the king's palace and fills the trees with candy and books and toys and all sorts of good things. When night comes, the children dress up in warm clothes and go to the forest to gather gifts for their friends. The forest is so big that there is room for everyone to wander around and choose gifts for all their friends in secret. No one ever thinks of taking a present for himself.

So Christmastime is a great holiday in the land, as it is in all the best places in the world. They have been celebrating it this way for hundreds of years.

But one time, many years ago, the children of The Great Walled Country had a very strange Christmas. Early that year, a visitor came to the land. He was the first stranger in a long, long time who had been able to get over the wall of ice.

The king and queen invited the visitor to the palace. He was a great explorer, and talked for hours about all the places he had

seen. Then he asked the king all about The Great Walled Country. He wanted to know about their customs and holidays. When the king told him about their Christmas, the young explorer laughed.

"That is all very well," he said, "but I should think that children who have Grandfather Christmas for a neighbor could find a better and easier way to get your presents. Why don't you each choose your own presents when you go into the forest? No one can tell what you want as well as you can."

The king thought this was a very wise idea, and so did the queen and the princes and all the members of the court. They all agreed that they had been very foolish never to have thought of this simple way of getting their Christmas gifts.

"If we do this," the queen said, "no one can ever complain of what he has or wish that someone had taken more pains to find out what he wanted."

"Yes," said the king. "In fact, I will make

a proclamation, and from now on we will follow the new plan."

So the proclamation was made. The plan seemed as wise to the children of the country as it had to the king and queen. Everyone had at some time been a little disappointed with their Christmas gifts. Now there would be no danger of that.

The stranger was soon gone from the country. The seasons passed until at last it was Christmastime again.

Now, on Christmas Eve the children always got together at the palace and sang carols until it was time to go into the forest.

On this particular night it seemed to the king that the music was not quite as merry, and the children's eyes did not shine as gladly as in other years. But there could be no good reason for this, since everyone was expecting a better time than usual, so he thought no more about it.

There was only one person at the palace that night who was not pleased with the new plan about the Christmas gifts. This was a boy named Peter, who lived not far from the palace with his sister Rose. Rose's legs were crippled and she could not walk. She spent her days in her chair by the window, looking out at the world beyond their little house.

Peter took good care of his sister and tried to make her happy in every way he could. On Christmas he had always gone to the forest and returned loaded with pretty things for Rose. And although she was not able to go after presents for her brother, he did not mind. He always got plenty of gifts from his friends.

But now, Peter wondered, what about Rose? By the king's order, they could only go out once and take gifts for themselves. All of Peter's friends were busy planning what they would pick, but his poor sister could not go one step toward the forest.

After thinking for a long time, Peter knew there was only one thing he could do.

At ten o'clock, the children made their

way in starlight that was so bright it almost showed their shadows on the sparkling snow. As soon as they came to the edge of the forest, they set out separately in the old way, even though now there was no reason they had to have secrets from one another.

Ten minutes later, if you had been in the forest, you would have seen the children standing with tears running down their cheeks. For as they searched the low-bending branches of the evergreen trees, they saw nothing hanging from them that could not be seen every day of the year. Had Grandfather Christmas forgotten them, or had there been some dreadful accident that kept him away?

As the children went trooping out of the forest after hours of searching, some of them came upon Peter. He was carrying a bag that seemed to be full to overflowing. When he saw them, he cried, "Isn't this wonderful? I think Grandfather Christmas has never been so good to us before."

"Why, what do you mean?" cried his

friends. "There are no presents in the forest."

"No presents?" said Peter. "I have a bag full of them." But he did not open the bag to show them. He did not want the others to see he had not obeyed the king's order. The presents in his bag were all for Rose and not for himself.

Then the other children begged him to tell them in what part of the forest he had found his presents. He turned and pointed to the place where he had been.

"I left many more than I took," he said. "There they are! I can see some of the things shining on the trees even from here."

But when the others followed his footprints in the snow to the place he pointed out, they still saw nothing. They thought that Peter must be walking in his sleep and dreaming that he had found presents. Perhaps he had filled his bag with the cones from the evergreen trees.

On Christmas Day there was sadness all through The Great Walled Country. But those who came to the house of Peter and his sister saw plenty of books and dolls and beautiful toys piled up around Rose's chair. When they asked where these things came from, they were told, "Why, from the Christmas-tree forest." But how could that be? There had been no gifts on the trees!

The king chose three of the princes to go visit Grandfather Christmas. He was the only one who could tell them what had happened.

It was very hard work to climb the great

wall of ice that lay between their country and the place where Grandfather Christmas lived, but at last the princes reached the top. When they came to the other side of the wall, they were looking down into the chimney of his house. One by one they slipped down the chimney and found themselves in the very room where Grandfather Christmas lay sound asleep.

Grandfather Christmas always slept one hundred days after his Christmas work was over. The only way they could wake him up was to turn the hands of the clock around two hundred times. After the clock had struck twelve times two hundred hours, Grandfather Christmas thought it was time for his nap to be over. He sat up in bed, rubbing his eyes.

"Oh, sir!" cried the prince who was in charge. "We have come from The Great Walled Country. The king wants to know why you forgot us this Christmas, and left no presents in the forest."

"I never forget you," said Grandfather

Christmas. "The presents were there. You did not see them, that's all."

The children told him that they had searched long and carefully and in the whole forest they had found not one thing that could be called a Christmas gift.

"Indeed!" said Grandfather Christmas. "And what about Peter, the boy with the crippled sister? Didn't he find presents?"

Then the princes were silent, for they had heard about the gifts at Peter's house.

"You had better go home," said Grandfather Christmas, "and let me finish my nap. The presents were there, but they were never intended for children who were looking only for themselves. I am not surprised that you did not see them. Remember that not everything a wise traveler tells you is wise." And he turned over and went back to sleep.

Back at The Great Walled Country, the princes told the king what they had learned. The king did not tell the other children what Grandfather Christmas had said. But, when the next December came, he made another proclamation, ordering everyone to seek gifts for others in the Christmas-tree forest in the old way.

So that is what they have been doing ever since. And in order that they do not forget what happened (in case anyone should ever ask for another change), the king reads to them every year from their Big Book the story of the sad Christmas when they had no gifts.

The Elves
and the Shoemaker

Retold by Freya Littledale

There was once a good shoemaker who
became very poor.

At last he had only one piece of leather to
make one pair of shoes.

"Well," said the shoemaker to his wife, "I
will cut the leather tonight and make the
shoes in the morning."

The next morning he went to his table,
and he couldn't believe what he saw. The
leather was polished. The sewing was done.
And there was a fine pair of shoes! Not one
stitch was out of place.

"Do you see what I see?" asked the shoemaker.

"Indeed I do," said his wife. "I see a fine pair of shoes."

"But who could have made them?" the shoemaker said.

"It's just like magic!" said his wife.

At that very moment a man came in with a top hat and cane. "Those shoes look right for me," said the man.

And so they were. They were right from heel to toe.

"How much do they cost?"

"One gold coin," said the shoemaker.

"I'll give you two," said the man.

And he went on his way with a smile on his face and the new shoes on his feet.

"Well, well," said the shoemaker, "now I can buy leather for two pairs of shoes." And he cut the leather that night so he could make the shoes in the morning.

The next morning the shoemaker woke up, and he found two pairs of ladies' shoes. They were shining in the sunlight.

"Who is making these shoes?" said the shoemaker. "They are the best shoes in the world."

At that very moment two ladies came in. They looked exactly alike. "My, what pretty shoes!" said the ladies. "They will surely fit us."

And the ladies were right.

They gave the shoemaker four gold coins and away they went . . . *clickety-clack, clickety-clack* in their pretty shoes.

And so it went. Every night the shoemaker cut the leather. Every morning the shoes were made. And every day more people came to buy his beautiful shoes. Just before Christmas the shoemaker said, "Whoever is making these shoes is making us very happy."

"And rich," said his wife.

"Let us stay up and see who it is," the shoemaker said.

"Good," said his wife.

So they hid behind some coats, and they waited and waited and waited.

When the clock struck twelve, in came the two little elves.

"Elves," cried the shoemaker.

"Shh!" said his wife.

At once the elves hopped up on the table and set to work.

Tap-tap went their hammers.

Snip-snap went their scissors.

Stitch-stitch went their needles.

Their tiny fingers moved so fast the shoemaker and his wife could hardly believe their eyes.

The elves sewed and they hammered and they didn't stop until all the shoes were finished. There were little shoes and big ones. There were white ones and black ones and brown ones.

The elves lined them all in a row. Then they jumped down from the table. They ran across the room and out the door.

The next morning, the wife said, "The elves have made us very happy. I want to make them happy, too. They need new clothes to keep warm. So I'll make them pants and shirts and coats. And I'll knit them socks and hats. You can make them each a pair of shoes."

"Yes, yes!" said the shoemaker. And they went right to work.

On Christmas Eve the shoemaker left no leather on the table. He left all the pretty gifts instead.

Then he and his wife hid behind the coats to see what the elves would do.

When the clock struck twelve, in came the elves, ready to set to work.

But when they looked at the table and saw the fine clothes, they laughed and clapped their hands.

"How happy they are!" said the shoemaker's wife.

"Shhh," said her husband. The elves put on the clothes, looked in the mirror, and began to sing:

What fine and handsome elves are we,
No longer cobblers will we be.
From now on we'll dance and play,
Into the woods and far away.

They hopped over the table and jumped over the chairs.

They skipped all around the room, danced out the door, and were never seen again.

But from that night on everything always went well for the good shoemaker and his wife.

The Tree
That Trimmed Itself

by Carolyn Sherwin Bailey
Adapted by Eva Moore

The forest was very still and cold. It was Christmas Eve, the night of wonder.

A young pine tree sighed as the wind blew through its branches. "How I wish that I could be a real Christmas tree tonight covered with shiny, bright ornaments!"

Suddenly something happened there in the woods. Floating down among the outspread branches of the pine tree came snowflakes, shaped like shining crystals.

More and then still more of the snow

stars fell, until every twig of every branch of the tree held its white stars. They were more beautiful than any ornaments made for trimming a Christmas tree.

But still the young pine tree longed for more. "I wish that I might hear the Christmas chimes!" it sighed in the wind.

Then the night grew colder and colder. The frost came through the forest and stopped beside the pine tree. It hung sharp, hard icicles to the tips of all its branches. Whenever the wind touched the tree the icicles tinkled and rang like a chime of tiny Christmas bells.

At the same time the stars shone out in the darkness and dropped their beams of light onto the ice-covered branches of the young pine tree. One star seemed to leave the sky and rest on the topmost branch. Now the pine tree was lighted as brightly as if it carried a hundred sparkling lights. But still it did not feel complete.

"I am not yet a Christmas tree!" it sighed. "I wish that I might hold gifts

among my branches." And it seemed as if this wish could never come true, for where could Christmas gifts be found in the wintry forest?

Christmas Eve changed to the very early dawning of Christmas Day. Still the pine tree wore its snow stars. Its icicle chimes rang in the clear, cold air, and the light of the sky shone in its branches. Then, out from the shelter of a nest among the tree's roots crept a mouse, cold and hungry.

But wait! Hanging to the pine tree, just above the nest of the mouse, was a bunch of berries on a trailing vine. The vine had twisted itself around the trunk of the tree in the summertime and now, in the deep winter, its bright berries hung there, a gift on Christmas morning for the hungry little mouse.

And out from a hole in the pine tree's trunk came a squirrel. He, too, was hungry. He ran along the branch until he came to the part of the tree where it had held tightly, in spite of the winter winds, a fat brown pinecone, full of seeds.

The squirrel held the cone in his paws, and munched the seeds with his sharp teeth. No better Christmas gift could have come to the squirrel than that fat pinecone.

"Merry Christmas!" called the children, running to the woods later on the morning of Christmas Day.

"Merry Christmas, little pine tree," a girl said. "We have brought a gift for your snow bird. We heard him calling yesterday." The girl held out a bundle of ripe grain tied with a red ribbon. She reached up as far as she could to hang the bundle on the green branches of the little pine tree.

In the next moment, the snow bird came out from a nest hidden deep inside the tree and began to eat the grain.

"Look," the girl said to her friends. "The little pine tree must have held that nest very closely all winter to give the snow bird a Christmas cradle!"

And the little pine tree stood straight and happy there in the woods on Christmas morning, for all of its wishes had come true. It had trimmed itself with stars, and heard the chimes. Best of all, it had given its gifts to its friends of the forest.

The Littles' Christmas

by John Peterson
pictures by Roberta Carter Clark

The Littles are a family of tiny people — the tallest is just six inches tall — who live inside the walls of a house belonging to Mr. and Mrs. Bigg and their son, Henry. The Littles have their own secret apartment in the walls, but sometimes they come out into the rooms of the house and use things when the Biggs are asleep or away.

One Christmas after a very exciting adventure in a tiny town called Trash City, members of the Littles family meet in the Biggs's living room to celebrate Christmas together. Even Cousin Dinky, a glider pilot, and his wife, Della, have flown in to be there. Uncle Nick, a retired soldier who had fought mice in Trash City, is recovering from a bad accident and everyone is feeling especially happy on this Christmas Day.

It was two o'clock Christmas morning. The Biggs and their visiting relatives were asleep. Near the Christmas tree in the Biggs's living room stood a dollhouse. It was a present from Mrs. Bigg to her niece, Mary.

At the moment the dollhouse was the scene of a Christmas party. All of the Littles were gathered there. Tiny lamps lighted the rooms. In the living room of the dollhouse stood a toy Christmas tree. There were presents under the tree. Wrapping paper was scattered about the floor.

Near the tiny tree, and lying on a miniature couch, was Uncle Nick. His friends Tip and Winkie McDust sat near him. They were laughing. Uncle Nick was smiling.

"Are you sure you'll be all right here?" asked Uncle Pete. He spoke to Uncle Nick.

"Don't worry about me, Peter," said Uncle Nick. "Enjoy the party." Then: "Let's open some more presents."

"What a wonderful idea Nick had," said Granny Little. "Using the dollhouse for a party."

"It's our only chance to see the dollhouse Mrs. Bigg made," said Mrs. Little. "Her niece will be taking it home with her when she leaves."

Just then Aunt Lily came in. She was carrying some of her fruitcake. "More goodies for the good people," she said. "The eggnog is coming right up."

Lucy picked up a present from under the tree. "It's for you, Tom," she said. "From Uncle Nick."

"Oh, wow!" Tom said. "I can hardly wait to open it. Uncle Nick gives super presents."

In a few moments the boy removed the wrapping paper from the present.

"It's Uncle Nick's *sword*!" said Tom. He ran to Uncle Nick, who looked startled.

"Is something wrong, Uncle Nick?" asked Tom.

"Nick — you gave Tom your sword!" said Uncle Pete. "What on earth for? You'll need it."

"Well, I . . . I . . ." stammered Uncle Nick.

"Oh my stars!" said Aunt Lily. She covered her face with her hands. "What have I done?"

Everyone turned to Aunt Lily.

"Tom," said Aunt Lily, "I wrapped up that present for you when your uncle thought he was going to die. Nick *insisted* that he wanted to leave you his sword. Now, of course, he . . ."

"Oh." Tom looked disappointed.

". . . and I forgot to unwrap it after he decided to go on living a little longer," Aunt Lily went on. "I'm sorry."

"That's okay," Tom said. "I . . . I understand." He held out the sword to Uncle Nick.

"No, Tom — no!" said Uncle Nick. "I really want you to have it. I just decided."

"Golly," said Tom. "Wow! This is the best present I ever had." He looked the sword over.

"Nick," said Granny Little. "That was sweet."

Uncle Nick laughed. "Guess what!" he said. "I just discovered it's more fun to give things away while you're still around." He smiled at everyone. "You know — it's great to be alive!"

"That reminds me of a song," said Cousin Dinky. He grinned as he reached for his guitar.

"Oh, no!" said Uncle Pete under his breath. "Dinky's going to ruin the party."

(Cousin Dinky loved to sing. He wrote songs about his adventures. The trouble was he had a terrible singing voice. Only Granny Little, who was hard of hearing, liked to hear Cousin Dinky sing.)

"Oh, good!" said Granny Little. "Quiet everyone! I want to hear every word."

Cousin Dinky sat on a stool, strummed his guitar, and sang:

It's great to be alive!
When I'm flying through the skies
Thinking I may crash
In a city made of trash
It's *great* to be alive!

On other sorts of days
In other kinds of ways
When I'm all alone and still
And suddenly my heart fills
with — *It's great to be alive!*

And when Christmas Day is come
And here is everyone
My family and my friends
May the story never end
It's *great* to be alive!

"Why, Dinky," said Della, "I never heard that song before. You made it up just now."

"I like it," Uncle Nick said. "Especially that line: 'It's great to be alive!'"

Tom tapped Uncle Pete on the shoulder. "Okay, Uncle Pete," he said. "The song is over. You can take your fingers out of your ears now."

Conversation Between
Mr. and Mrs. Santa Claus

"Are the reindeer in the rain, dear?"
Asked Mrs. Santa Claus.
"No. I put them in the barn, dear,
To dry their little paws."

"Is the sleigh, sir, put away, sir?
In the barn beside the deer?"
"Yes, I'm going to get it ready
To use again next year."

"And the pack, dear, is it back, dear?"
"Yes. It's empty of its toys,
And tomorrow I'll start filling it,
For next year's girls and boys."

Rowena Bennett

Credits

"Counting the Days" by James Tippett from CRICKETY CRICKET! THE BEST LOVED POEMS OF JAMES S. TIPPETT. Copyright 1933 and renewed © 1973 by Martha K. Tippett. Reprinted by permission of HarperCollins Publishers.

Text from THE LOST CHRISTMAS by Howard Knotts. Copyright © 1978 by Howard R. Knotts. Reprinted by permission of Harcourt Brace & Company.

"Words from an Old Spanish Carol" by Ruth Sawyer. From THE LONG CHRISTMAS by Ruth Sawyer. Copyright 1941 by Ruth Sawyer. Used by permission of Viking Penguin, a division of Penguin Books USA, Inc.

"The Cat in the Manger" by Wendie Old. Copyright © 1988 by Wendie C. Old. From Cricket Magazine, December 1988.

"The Story of Old Befana" from AROUND THE CHURCH/AROUND THE YEAR: UNITARIAN UNIVERSALISM FOR CHILDREN KINDERGARTEN TO GRADE 2 by Jan Evans-Tiller. Copyright © 1990 by The Unitarian Universalist Association, 25 Beacon Street, Boston, MA 02108. All rights reserved.

APPLE TREE CHRISTMAS by Trinka Hakes Noble. Copyright © 1984 by Trinka Hakes Noble. Published by Dial Books for Young Readers, a division of Penguin Books USA, Inc.

"Presents" by Marchette Chute. Copyright 1932 by Marchette Chute.

"Letter from Father Christmas" by J.R.R. Tolkien. From THE FATHER CHRISTMAS LETTERS by J.R.R. Tolkien. Published by HarperCollins UK.

From THE ELVES AND THE SHOEMAKER retold by Freya Littledale. Copyright © 1975 by Freya Littledale. Reprinted by permission of Scholastic Inc.

"The Littles' Christmas" from THE LITTLES AND THE TRASH TINIES by John Peterson. Copyright © 1977 by John Peterson. Reprinted by permission of Scholastic Inc.

"Conversation between Mr. and Mrs. Santa Claus" by Rowena Bennett. From JACK AND JILL. Copyright © 1947 by Curtis Publishing Co. Used by permission of Children's Better Health Institute, Benjamin Franklin Literary and Medical Society, Inc., Indianapolis, Indiana.